Edward Young

The Revenge

Outlook

Edward Young

The Revenge

1. Auflage | ISBN: 978-3-73262-000-5

Erscheinungsort: Frankfurt am Main, Deutschland

Erscheinungsjahr: 2018

Outlook Verlag GmbH, Frankfurt.

THE REVENGE.

A Tragedy,

IN FIVE ACTS.

1

BY DR. YOUNG.

CORRECTLY GIVEN,

AS PERFORMED AT THE THEATRES ROYAL.

With Remarks.

London:

Printed by D. S. Maurice, Fenchurch-street;

SOLD BY

T. HUGHES, 35, LUDGATE STREET, AND J. BYSH,
52, PATERNOSTER ROW;

REMARKS.

This tragedy is the dramatic master-piece of it's valuable author, but at first was not so successful as Busiris and his other plays. Though similar, in some degree, to the story of Shakspeare's *Othello*, the motives for resentment in Zanga are of a more noble and consistent nature, and the credulous object of his deadly hatred more excusable and more pitied in yielding to it's subtlety.

There is great scope for talent in the character of Zanga; but the whining nonsense of Alonzo and Carlos would tire in any hands.

We have inserted, on page 59, a narrative said to have really happened in Spain a few years before this piece was written;—it is so nearly followed by Dr. Young in his admirable *Revenge*, as to leave no doubt of having formed it's ground-work.

DRAMATIS PERSONÆ.

Covent Garden, 1814.

Don Alonzo	Mr. Conway.
Don Carlos	Mr. Hamerton.
Don Alvarez	Mr. Murray.
Don Manuel	Mr. Creswell.
Zanga	Mr. Young.
Officers	Messrs. Brown, Grant, &c.
Leonora	Mrs. Egerton.
Isabella	Miss Logan.

SCENE—Spain.

3

THE REVENGE.

ACT THE FIRST.

SCENE I.   BATTLEMENTS, WITH A SEA PROSPECT.

Enter Zanga.

Zan. Whether first nature, or long want of peace,
Has wrought my mind to this, I cannot tell;
But horrors now are not displeasing to me: [*thunder.*
I like this rocking of the battlements.
Rage on, ye winds; burst, clouds; and, waters, roar!
You bear a just resemblance of my fortune,
And suit the gloomy habit of my soul.

Enter Isabella.

Who's there? My love!

Isa. Why have you left my bed?
Your absence more affrights me than the storm.

Zan. The dead alone in such a night can rest,
And I indulge my meditation here.
Woman, away. I choose to be alone.

Isa. I know you do, and therefore will not leave you;
Excuse me, Zanga, therefore dare not leave you.
Is this a night for walks of contemplation?
Something unusual hangs upon your heart,
And I will know it: by our loves, I will.
Ask I too much to share in your distress?

Zan. In tears? thou fool! then hear me, and be plung'd
In hell's abyss, if ever it escape thee.
To strike thee with astonishment at once—
I hate Alonzo. First recover that,
And then thou shalt hear further.

Isa. Hate Alonzo!
I own, I thought Alonzo most your friend,
And that he lost the master in that name.

Zan. Hear then. 'Tis twice three years since that great man
(Great let me call him, for he conquer'd me)
Made me the captive of his arm in fight.
He slew my father, and threw chains o'er me,
While I with pious rage pursu'd revenge.
I then was young; he plac'd me near his person,
And thought me not dishonour'd by his service.
One day (may that returning day be night,
The stain, the curse, of each succeeding year!)
For something, or for nothing, in his pride
He struck me. (While I tell it, do I live?)
He smote me on the cheek—I did not stab him,
For that were poor revenge—E'er since, his folly
Has strove to bury it beneath a heap
Of kindnesses, and thinks it is forgot.
Insolent thought! and like a second blow!
Affronts are innocent, where men are worthless;
And such alone can wisely drop revenge.

Isa. But with more temper, Zanga, tell your story;
To see your strong emotions startles me.

Zan. Yes, woman, with the temper that befits it.

5

Has the dark adder venom? So have I
When trod upon. Proud Spaniard, thou shalt feel me!
For from that day, that day of my dishonour,
From that day have I curs'd the rising sun,
Which never fail'd to tell me of my shame.
From that day have I bless'd the coming night,
Which promis'd to conceal it; but in vain;
The blow return'd for ever in my dream.
Yet on I toil'd, and groan'd for an occasion
Of ample vengeance; none has yet arriv'd.
Howe'er, at present, I conceive warm hopes
Of what may wound him sore in his ambition,
Life of his life, and dearer than his soul.
By nightly march he purpos'd to surprise
The Moorish camp; but I have taken care
They shall be ready to receive his favour.
Failing in this, a cast of utmost moment,
Would darken all the conquests he has won.

Isa. Just as I enter'd, an express arriv'd.

Zan. To whom?

Isa. His friend, don Carlos.

Zan. Be propitious,
Oh! Mahomet, on this important hour,
And give at length my famish'd soul revenge!
What is revenge, but courage to call in
Our honour's debts, and wisdom to convert
Others' self-love into our own protection?
But see, the morning dawn breaks in upon us;
I'll seek don Carlos, and inquire my fate.   [*exeunt.*

6

SCENE II. THE PALACE.

Enter Don Manuel and Don Carlos.

Man. My lord don Carlos, what brings your express?

Car. Alonzo's glory, and the Moor's defeat.
The field is strew'd with twice ten thousand slain,
Though he suspects his measures were betray'd,
He'll soon arrive. Oh, how I long t'embrace
The first of heroes, and the best of friends!
I lov'd fair Leonora long before
The chance of battle gave me to the Moors,
From whom so late Alonzo set me free;
And while I groan'd in bondage, I deputed
This great Alonzo, whom her father honours,
To be my gentle advocate in love,
To stir her heart, and fan its fires for me.

Man. And what success?

Car. Alas, the cruel maid—
Indeed her father, who, though high in court,
And pow'rful with the king, has wealth at heart
To heal his devastations from the Moors,
Knowing I'm richly freighted from the east,
My fleet now sailing in the sight of Spain,
(Heav'n guard it safe through such a dreadful storm!)
Caresses me, and urges her to wed.

Man. Her aged father, see,
Leads her this way.

Car. She looks like radiant truth,
Brought forward by the hand of hoary time—

You to the port with speed; 'tis possible
Some vessel is arriv'd. Heav'n grant it bring
Tidings which Carlos may receive with joy!   [*exit D. M.*

Enter Don Alvarez and Leonora.

Alv. Don Carlos, I am lab'ring in your favour
With all a parent's soft authority,
And earnest counsel.

Car. Angels second you!
For all my bliss or mis'ry hangs on it.

Alv. Daughter, the happiness of life depends
On our discretion, and a prudent choice.
Look into those they call unfortunate,
And, closer view'd, you'll find they are unwise:
Some flaw in their own conduct lies beneath.
Don Carlos is of ancient, noble blood,
And then his wealth might mend a prince's fortune.
For him the sun is lab'ring in the mines,
A faithful slave, and turning earth to gold:
His keels are freighted with that sacred pow'r,
By which e'en kings and emperors are made.
Sir, you have my good wishes, and I hope
My daughter is not indispos'd to hear you.   [*exit.*

Car. Oh, Leonora! why art thou in tears?
Because I am less wretched than I was?
Before your father gave me leave to woo you,
Hush'd was your bosom, and your eye serene.

Leon. Think you my father too indulgent to me,
That he claims no dominion o'er my tears?

8

A daughter sure may be right dutiful,
Whose tears alone are free from a restraint.

   Car. Had I known this before it had been well:
I had not then solicited your father
To add to my distress;
Have I not languish'd prostrate at thy feet?
Have I not liv'd whole days upon thy sight?
Have I not seen thee where thou hast not been?
And, mad with the idea, clasp'd the wind,
And doated upon nothing?

   Leon. Court me not,
Good Carlos, by recounting of my faults,
And telling how ungrateful I have been.
Alas, my lord, if talking would prevail,
I could suggest much better arguments
Than those regards you threw away on me;
Your valour, honour, wisdom, prais'd by all.
But bid physicians talk our veins to temper,
And with an argument new-set a pulse;
Then think, my lord, of reas'ning into love.

   Car. Must I despair then? do not shake me thus:
My temper-beaten heart is cold to death.
Ah, turn, and let me warm me in thy beauties.
Heav'ns! what a proof I gave, but two nights past,
Of matchless love! To fling me at thy feet,
I slighted friendship, and I flew from fame;
Nor heard the summons of the next day's battle:
But darting headlong to thy arms, I left
The promis'd fight, I left Alonzo too,
To stand the war, and quell a world alone.   [*trumpets.*

Leon. The victor comes. My lord, I must withdraw.   [*exit.*

Enter Don Alonzo.

Car. Alonzo!

Alon. Carlos!—I am whole again;
Clasp'd in thy arms, it makes my heart entire.

Car. Whom dare I thus embrace? The conqueror
Of Afric.

Alon. Yes, much more—Don Carlos' friend.
The conquest of the world would cost me dear,
Should it beget one thought of distance in thee.
I rise in virtues to come nearer to thee.
I conquer with Don Carlos in mine eye,
And thus I claim my victory's reward.   [*embraces him.*

Car. A victory indeed! your godlike arm
Has made one spot the grave of Africa;
Such numbers fell! and the survivors fled
As frighted passengers from off the strand,
When the tempestuous sea comes roaring on them.

Alon. 'Twas Carlos conquer'd, 'twas his cruel chains
Inflam'd me to a rage unknown before,
And threw my former actions far behind.

Car. I love fair Leonora. How I love her!
Yet still I find (I know not how it is)
Another heart, another soul, for thee.

Enter Zanga.

10

Zan. Manuel, my lord, returning from the port,
On business both of moment and of haste,
Humbly begs leave to speak in private with you.

Car. In private!—Ha!—Alonzo, I'll return;
No business can detain me long from thee.　　　　[*exit.*

Zan. My lord Alonzo, I obey'd your orders.

Alon. Will the fair Leonora pass this way?

Zan. She will, my lord, and soon.

Alon. Come near me, Zanga;
For I dare open all my heart to thee.
Never was such a day of triumph known!—
There's not a wounded captive in my train,
That slowly follow'd my proud chariot wheels,
With half a life, and beggary, and chains.
But is a god to me: I am most wretched.—
In his captivity, thou know'st, don Carlos,
My friend (and never was a friend more dear)
Deputed me his advocate in love,
To talk to Leonora's heart, and make
A tender party in her thoughts for him.
What did I do?—I lov'd myself. Indeed,
One thing there is might lessen my offence
(If such offence admits of being lessen'd);
I thought him dead; for (by what fate I know not)
His letters never reach'd me.

Zan. Thanks to Zanga,　　　　[*aside.*
Who thence contriv'd that evil which has happen'd.

11

Alon. Yes, curs'd of heav'n! I lov'd myself, and now,
In a late action, rescu'd from the Moors,
I have brought home my rival in my friend.

Zan. We hear, my lord, that in that action too,
Your interposing arm preserv'd his life.

Alon. It did—with more than the expense of mine:
For, oh, this day is mention'd for their nuptials.
But see, she comes; I'll take my leave, and die.   [*retires.*

Zan. Hadst thou a thousand lives, thy death would please me.
Unhappy fate! my country overcome!
My six years' hope of vengeance quite expir'd!—
Would nature were—I will not fall alone:
But others' groans shall tell the world my death.   [*exit.*

Enter Leonora.

Alon. When nature ends with anguish like to this,
Sinners shall take their last leave of the sun,
And bid his light adieu.

Leon. The mighty conqueror
Dismay'd! I thought you gave the foe your sorrows.

Alon. Oh, cruel insult! are those tears your sport,
Which nothing but a love for you could draw?
Afric I quell'd, in hope by that to purchase
Your leave to sigh unscorn'd; but I complain not;
'Twas but a world, and you are—Leonora.

Leon. That passion which you boast of is your guilt,

A treason to your friend. You think mean of me,
To plead your crimes as motives of my love.

Alon. You, madam, ought to thank those crimes you blame!
'Tis they permit you to be thus inhuman,
Without the censure both of earth and heav'n—
I fondly thought a last look might be kind.
Farewell for ever.—This severe behaviour
Has, to my comfort, made it sweet to die.

Leon. Farewell for ever! Sweet to die! Oh, heav'n!
Alonzo, stay; you must not thus escape me;
But hear your guilt at large.

Alon. Oh, Leonora!
What could I do?—In duty to my friend,
I saw you; and to see is to admire.
For Carlos did I plead, and most sincerely.
Witness the thousand agonies it cost me.
You know I did; I sought but your esteem;
If that is guilt, an angel had been guilty.

Leon. If from your guilt none suffer'd but yourself,
It might be so—Farewell.   [*going.*

Alon. Who suffers with me?

Leon. Enjoy your ignorance, and let me go.

Alon. What mean these tears?

Leon. I weep by chance; nor have my tears a meaning.
But, oh, when first I saw Alonzo's tears,
I knew their meaning well!

[Alonzo falls on his knees, and takes her hand.

Alon. Heav'ns! what is this? that excellence, for which
Desire was planted in the heart of man;
Virtue's supreme reward on this side heav'n;
The cordial of my soul—and this destroys me—
Indeed, I flatter'd me that thou didst hate.

Leon. Alonzo, pardon me the injury
Of loving you. I struggled with my passion,
And struggled long: let that be some excuse.

Alon. Unkind! you know I think your love a blessing
Beyond all human blessings! 'tis the price
Of sighs and groans, and a whole year of dying.
But, oh, the curse of curses!—Oh, my friend!—

Leon. Alas!

Alon. What says my love? speak, Leonora.

Leon. Was it for you, my lord, to be so quick
In finding out objections to our love?
Think you so strong my love, or weak my virtue,
It was unsafe to leave that part to me?

Alon. Is not the day then fix'd for your espousals?

Leon. Indeed, my father once had thought that way;
But marking how the marriage pain'd my heart,
Long he stood doubtful; but at lastresolv'd
Your counsel, which determines him in all,
Should finish the debate.

Alon. Oh, agony!
Must I not only lose her, but be made
Myself the instrument? not only die,
But plunge the dagger in my heart myself?
This is refining on calamity.

Leon. What, do you tremble lest you should be mine?
For what else can you tremble? not for that
My father places in your power to alter.

Alon. What's in my pow'r? oh, yes, to stab my friend!

Leon. To stab your friend were barbarous indeed!
Spare him—and murder me.

Alon. First perish all!
No, Leonora, I am thine for ever.   [*embraces her.*

Leon. Hold, Alonzo,
And hear a maid whom doubly thou hast conquer'd.
I love thy virtue as I love thy person,

And I adore thee for the pains it gave me;
But as I felt the pains, I'll reap the fruit;
I'll shine out in my turn, and show the world
Thy great example was not lost upon me.
Nay, never shrink; take back the bright example
You lately lent; Oh, take it while you may,
While I can give it you, and be immortal!   [*exit.*

Alon. She's gone, and I shall see that face no more;
But pine in absence, and till death adore.
When with cold dew my fainting brow is hung,
And my eyes darken, from my falt'ring tongue

Her name will tremble in a feeble moan,
And love with fate divide my dying groan.   [*exit.*

ACT THE SECOND.

SCENE I.   THE SAME.

Enter Don Manuel and Zanga.

Zan. If this be true, I cannot blame your pain
For wretched Carlos; 'tis but humane in you.
But when arriv'd your dismal news?

Man. This hour.

Zan. What, not a vessel sav'd?

Man. All, all, the storm
Devour'd; and now o'er his late envy'd fortune
The dolphins bound, and wat'ry mountains roar,
Triumphant in his ruin.

Zan. Is Alvarez
Determin'd to deny his daughter to him.
That treasure was on shore; must that too join
The common wreck?

Man. Alvarez pleads, indeed,
That Leonora's heart is disinclin'd,
And pleads that only; so it was this morning,
When he coucurr'd: the tempest broke the match;
And sunk his favour, when it sunk the gold.
The love of gold is double in his heart;

The vice of age, and of Alvarez too.

Zan. How does don Carlos bear it?

Man. Like a man
Whose heart feels most a human heart can feel,
And reasons best a human head can reason.

Zan. But is he then in absolute despair?

Man. Never to see his Leonora more.
And, quite to quench all future hope, Alvarez
Urges Alonzo to espouse his daughter
This very day; for he has learn'd their loves.

Zan. Ha! was not that receiv'd with ecstasy
By don Alonzo?

Man. Yes, at first; but soon
A damp came o'er him, it would kill his friend.

Zan. Not if his friend consented: and since now
He can't himself espouse her—

Man. Yet, to ask it
Has something shocking to a gen'rous mind;
At least, Alonzo's spirit startles at it.
Wide is the distance between our despair,
And giving up a mistress to another.
But I must leave you. Carlos wants support
In his severe affliction.   [*exit.*

Zan. Ha, it dawns!—
It rises to me, like a new-found world

To mariners long time distress'd at sea,
Sore from a storm, and all their viands spent;
Or like the sun just rising out of chaos,
Some dregs of ancient night not quite purg'd off.
But shall I finish it?—Hoa, Isabella!

Enter Isabella.

I thought of dying; better things come forward;
Vengeance is still alive! from her dark covert,
With all her snakes erect upon her crest,
She stalks in view, and fires me with her charms.
When, Isabella, arriv'd don Carlos here?

   Isa. Two nights ago.

   Zan. That was the very night
Before the battle—Mem'ry, set down that;
It has the essence of a crocodile,
Though yet but in the shell—I'll give it birth—
What time did he return?

   Isa. At midnight.

   Zan. So—
Say, did he see that night his Leonora?

   Isa. No, my good lord.

   Zan. No matter—tell me, woman,
Is not Alonzo rather brave than cautious,
Honest than subtle, above fraud himself,
Slow, therefore, to suspect it in another?

Isa. You best can judge; but so the world thinks of him.

Zan. Why, that was well—go, fetch my tablets hither.

                                         [*exit Isabella.*

Two nights ago my father's sacred shade
Thrice stalk'd around my bed, and smil'd upon me:
He smil'd, a joy then little understood—
It must be so—and if so, it is vengeance
Worth waking of the dead for.

        Re-enter Isabella, with the tablets; Zanga writes,
                then reads as to himself.

Thus it stands—
The father's fix'd—Don Carlos cannot wed—
Alonzo may—but that will hurt his friend—
Nor can he ask his leave—or, if he did,
He might not gain it—It is hard to give
Our own consent to ills, though we must bear them.
Were it not then a master-piece worth all
The wisdom I can boast, first to persuade
Alonzo to request it of his friend,
His friend to grant—then from that very grant,
The strongest proof of friendship man can give
(And other motives), to work out a cause
Of jealousy, to rack Alonzo's peace?
I have turn'd o'er the catalogue of human woes,
Which sting the heart of man, and find none equal.
It is the hydra of calamities,
The sev'nfold death; the jealous are the damn'd.
Oh, jealousy, each other passion's calm
To thee, thou conflagration of the soul!
Thou king of torments, thou grand counterpoise
For all the transports beauty can inspire!

Isa. Alonzo comes this way.

Zan. Most opportunely.—
Withdraw.   [*exit Isabella.*

Enter Don Alonzo.

My lord, I give you joy.

Alon. Of what, good Zanga?

Zan. Is not the lovely Leonora yours?

Alon. What will become of Carlos?

Zan. He's your friend;
And since he can't espouse the fair himself,
Will take some comfort from Alonzo's fortune.

Alon. Alas, thou little know'st the force of love!
Love reigns a sultan with unrival'd sway;
Puts all relations, friendship's self to death,
If once he's jealous of it. I love Carlos;
Yet well I know what pangs I felt this morning
At his intended nuptials. For myself
I then felt pains, which now for him I feel.

Zan. You will not wed her then?

Alon. Not instantly.
Insult his broken heart the very moment!

Zan. I understand you: but you'll wed hereafter,

When your friend's gone, and his first pain assuag'd.

Alon. Am I to blame in that?

Zan. My lord, I love
Your very errors; they are born from virtue.
Your friendship (and what nobler passion claims
The heart?) does lead you blindfold to your ruin.
Consider, wherefore did Alvarez break
Don Carlos' match, and wherefore urge Alonzo's?
'Twas the same cause, the love of wealth. To-morrow
May see Alonzo in don Carlos' fortune;
A higher bidder is a better friend,
And there are princes sigh for Leonora.
When your friend's gone, you'll wed; why, then the cause
Which gives you Leonora now, will cease.
Carlos has lost her; should you lose her too,
Why, then you heap new torments on your friend,
By that respect which labour'd to relieve him—
'Tis well, he is disturb'd; it makes him pause.   [*aside.*

Alon. Think'st thou, my Zanga, should I ask don Carlos,
His goodness would consent that I should wed her?

Zan. I know, it would.

Alon. But then the cruelty
To ask it, and for me to ask it of him!

Zan. Methinks, you are severe upon your friend.
Who was it gave him liberty and life?

Alon. That is the very reason which forbids it.
Were I a stranger I could freely speak:

In me it so resembles a demand,
Exacting of a debt, it shocks my nature.

Zan. My lord, you know the sad alternative.
Is Leonora worth one pang or not?
It hurts not me, my lord, but as I love you:
Warmly as you I wish don Carlos well;
But I am likewise don Alonzo's friend:
There all the diff'rence lies between us two.
In me, my lord, you hear another self;
And, give me leave to add, a better too,
Clear'd from those errors, which, though caus'd by virtue,
Are such as may hereafter give you pain—
Don Lopez of Castile would not demur thus.

Alon. Perish the name! What, sacrifice the fair
To age and ugliness, because set in gold?
I'll to don Carlos, if my heart will let me.
I have not seen him since his sore affliction;
But shunn'd it, as too terrible to bear.
How shall I bear it now? I'm struck already.   [*exit.*

Zan. Half of my work is done. I must secure
Don Carlos, ere Alonzo speak with him.

[*he gives a message to a Servant, then returns.*

Proud, hated Spain, oft drench'd in Moorish blood!
Dost thou not feel a deadly foe within thee?
Shake not the tow'rs where'er I pass along,
Conscious of ruin, and their great destroyer?
Shake to the centre, if Alonzo's dear.
Look down, oh, holy prophet! see me torture

This Christian dog, this infidel, who dares

To smite thy votaries, and spurn thy law;
And yet hopes pleasure from two radiant eyes,
Which look as they were lighted up for thee!
Shall he enjoy thy paradise below?
Blast the bold thought, and curse him with her charms!
But see, the melancholy lover comes.

Enter Don Carlos.

Car. Hope, thou hast told me lies from day to day,
For more than twenty years; vile promiser!
None here are happy, but the very fool,
Or very wise: I am not fool enough
To smile in vanities, and hug a shadow;
Nor have I wisdom to elaborate
An artificial happiness from pains:
Ev'n joys are pains, because they cannot last.   [*sighs.*
How many lift the head, look gay and smile,
Against their consciences? And this we know,
Yet, knowing, disbelieve, and try again
What we have try'd, and struggle with conviction.
Each new experience gives the former credit;
And rev'rend grey threescore is but a voucher,
That thirty told us true.

Zan. My noble lord,
I mourn your fate: but are no hopes surviving?

Car. No hopes. Alvarez has a heart of steel.
'Tis fix'd—'tis past—'tis absolute despair!

Zan. You wanted not to have your heart made tender,
By your own pains, to feel a friend's distress.

Car. I understand you well. Alonzo loves;
I pity him.

Zan. I dare be sworn you do.
Yet he has other thoughts.

Car. What canst thou mean?

Zan. Indeed he has; and fears to ask a favour
A stranger from a stranger might request;
What costs you nothing, yet is all to him:
Nay, what indeed will to your glory add,
For nothing more than wishing your friend well.

Car. I pray be plain; his happiness is mine.

Zan. He loves to death; but so reveres his friend,
He can't persuade his heart to wed the maid
Without your leave, and that he fears to ask.
In perfect tenderness I urg'd him to it.
Knowing the deadly sickness of his heart,
Your overflowing goodness to your friend,
Your wisdom, and despair yourself to wed her,
I wrung a promise from him he would try:
And now I come, a mutual friend to both,
Without his privacy, to let you know it,
And to prepare you kindly to receive him.

Car. Ha! if he weds, I am undone indeed;
Not don Alvarez' self can then relieve me.

Zan. Alas, my lord, you know his heart is steel:
"'Tis fixed, 'tis past, 'tis absolute despair."

Car. Oh, cruel heav'n! and is it not enough
That I must never, never see her more?
Say, is it not enough that I must die;
But I must be tormented in the grave?—
Ask my consent!—Must I then give her to him?
Lead to his nuptial sheets the blushing maid?
Oh!—Leonora! never, never, never!

Zan. A storm of plagues upon him! he refuses.   [*aside.*

Car. What, wed her—and to-day?

Zan. To-day, or never.
To-morrow may some wealthier lover bring,
And then Alonzo is thrown out like you:
Then whom shall he condemn for his misfortune?
Carlos is an Alvarez to his love.

Car. Oh, torment! whither shall I turn?

Zan. To peace.

Car. Which is the way?

Zan. His happiness is yours——
I dare not disbelieve you.

Car. Kill my friend!
Or worse—Alas! and can there be a worse?
A worse there is: nor can my nature bear it.

Zan. You have convinc'd me 'tis a dreadful task.
I find Alonzo's quitting her this morning
For Carlos' sake, in tenderness to you,

Betray'd me to believe it less severe
Than I perceive it is.

    Car. Thou dost upbraid me.

    Zan. No, my good lord; but since you can't comply,
'Tis my misfortune that I mention'd it;
For had I not, Alonzo would indeed
Have died, as now, but not by your decree.

    Car. By my decree! Do I decree his death?
I do—Shall I then lead her to his arms?
Oh, which side shall I take? Be stabb'd, or—stab?
'Tis equal death! a choice of agonies!——
Ah, no!—all other agonies are ease
To one—O Leonora!—never, never!
Go, Zanga, go, defer the dreadful trial,
Though but a day; something, perchance, may happen
To soften all to friendship and to love.
Go, stop my friend, let me not see him now;
But save us from an interview of death.

    Zan. My lord, I'm bound in duty to obey you——
If I not bring him, may Alonzo prosper!   *[aside, exit.*

    Car. What is this world?—Thy school, oh, misery!
Our only lesson is to learn to suffer;
And he who knows not that was born for nothing.
But put it most severely—should I live—
Live long—alas, there is no length in time!
Nor in thy time, oh, man!—What's fourscore years
Nay, what, indeed, the age of time itself,
Since cut from out eternity's wide round?
Yet Leonora—she can make time long,

Its nature alter, as she alter'd mine.
   While in the lustre of her charms I lay,
   Whole summer suns roll'd unperceiv'd away;
   I years for days, and days for moments, told,
   And was surpris'd to hear that I grew old.
   Now fate does rigidly its dues regain,
   And ev'ry moment is an age of pain.

   Enter Zanga and Don Alonzo; Zanga stops Don Carlos.

   Zan. Is this don Carlos? this the boasted friend?
How can you turn your back upon his sadness?
Look on him, and then leave him if you can.

   Car. I cannot yield; nor can I bear his griefs.
Alonzo!   [*goes to him, and takes his hand.*

   Alon. Oh, Carlos!

   Car. Pray, forbear.

   Alon. Art thou undone, and shall Alonzo smile?
Alonzo, who, perhaps, in some degree
Contributed to cause thy dreadful fate?
I was deputed guardian of thy love;
But, oh! I lov'd myself! Pour down, afflictions!
On this devoted head; make me your mark;
And be the world by my example taught,
How sacred it should hold the name of friend.

   Car. You charge yourself unjustly: well I know
The only cause of my severe affliction.
Alvarez, curs'd Alvarez!—So much anguish
Felt for so small a failure, is one merit

Which faultless virtue wants. The crime was mine,
Who plac'd thee there, where only thou couldst fail;
Though well I knew that dreadful post of honour
I gave thee to maintain. Ah! who could bear
Those eyes unhurt? The wounds myself have felt
(Which wounds alone should cause me to condemn thee,)
They plead in thy excuse; for I too strove
To shun those fires, and found 'twas not in man.

    Alon. You cast in shades the failure of a friend,
And soften all; but think not you deceive me;
I know my guilt, and I implore your pardon,
As the sole glimpse I can obtain of peace.

    Car. Pardon for him, who but this morning threw
Fair Leonora from his heart, all bath'd
In ceaseless tears, and blushing for her love!
Who, like a rose-leaf wet with morning dew,
Would have stuck close, and clung for ever there!
But 'twas in thee, through fondness for thy friend,
To shut thy bosom against ecstacies;
For which, while this pulse beats, it beats to thee;
While this blood flows, it flows for my Alonzo,
And every wish is levell'd at thy joy.

    Zan. [*to Alon.*] My lord, my lord, this is your time to speak.

    Alon. [*to Zan.*] Because he's kind? It therefore is the worst;
Do I not see him quite possess'd with anguish,
And shall I pour in new? No, fond desire;
No, love: one pang at parting, and farewell,
I have no other love but Carlos now.

    Car. Alas! my friend, why with such eager grasp

Dost press my hand, and weep upon my cheek?

Alon. If, after death, our forms (as some believe)
Shall be transparent, naked every thought,
And friends meet friends, and read each other's hearts,
Thou'lt know one day that thou wast held most dear,
Farewell.

Car. Alonzo, stop—he cannot speak—   [*holds him.*
Lest it should grieve me—Shall I be outdone?
And lose in glory, as I lose in love?   [*aside.*
I take it much unkindly, my Alonzo,
You think so meanly of me not to speak,
When well I know your heart is near to bursting.
Have you forgot how you have bound me to you?
Your smallest friendship's liberty and life.

Alon. There, there it is, my friend; it cuts me there.
How dreadful is it to a generous mind
To ask, when sure it cannot be deny'd!

Car. How greatly thought! In all he towers above me.
                                              [*aside.*
Then you confess you would ask something of me?

Alon. No, on my soul.

Zan. [*to Alon.*] Then lose her.

Car. Glorious spirit!
Why, what a pang has he run through for this!
By heaven, I envy him his agonies.   [*aside.*
My Alonzo!
Since thy great soul disdains to make request,

Receive with favour that I make to thee.

Alon. What means my Carlos?

Car. Pray observe me well.
Fate and Alvarez tore her from my heart,
And, plucking up my love, they had well nigh
Pluck'd up life too, for they were twin'd together.
Of that no more—What now does reason bid?
I cannot wed—Farewell, my happiness!
But, O my soul, with care provide for hers!
In life, how weak, how helpless, is a woman!
Take then my heart in dowry with the fair,
Be thou her guardian, and thou must be mine;
Shut out the thousand pressing ills of life
With thy surrounding arms—Do this, and then
Set down the liberty and life thou gav'st me,
As little things, as essays of thy goodness,
And rudiments of friendship so divine.

Alon. There is a grandeur in thy goodness to me,
Which with thy foes would render thee ador'd.

Car. I do not part with her, I give her thee.

Alon. O, Carlos!

But think not words were ever made
For such occasions. Silence, tears, embraces,
Are languid eloquence; I'll seek relief
In absence from the pain of so much goodness,
There, thank the blest above, thy sole superiors,
Adore, and raise my thoughts of them by thee.   [*exit.*

Zan. Thus far success has crown'd my boldest hope.

My next care is to hasten these new nuptials,
And then my master-works begin to play.   [*aside.*
Why that was greatly done, without one sigh   [*to Car.*
To carry such a glory to its period.

    Car. Too soon thou praisest me. He's gone, and now
I must unsluice my over-burden'd heart,
And let it flow. I would not grieve my friend
With tears; nor interrupt my great design; Great,
sure, as ever human breast durst think of. But
now my sorrows, long with pain supprest,
    Burst their confinement with impetuous sway,
    O'er-swell all bounds, and bear e'en life away:
    So till the day was won, the Greek renown'd
    With anguish wore the arrow in his wound,
    Then drew the shaft from out his tortur'd side,
    Let gush the torrent of his blood, and dy'd.   [*exeunt.*

ACT THE THIRD.

SCENE I.

Enter Zanga.

Zan. O joy, thou welcome stranger! twice three years
I have not felt thy vital beam; but now
It warms my veins, and plays around my heart:
A fiery instinct lifts me from the ground,
And I could mount!—the spirits numberless
Of my dear countrymen, which yesterday
Left their poor bleeding bodies on the field,
Are all assembled here, and o'er-inform me.—
O, bridegroom! great indeed thy present bliss;
Yet even by me unenvy'd! for be sure
It is thy last, thy last smile, that which now
Sits on thy cheek; enjoy it while thou may'st;
Anguish, and groans, and death, bespeak to-morrow.

Enter Isabella.

My Isabella!

Isa. What commands my Moor?

Zan. My fair ally! my lovely minister!
'Twas well, Alvarez, by my arts impell'd
(To plunge don Carlos in the last despair,
And so prevent all future molestation),
Finish'd the nuptials soon as he resolv'd them;
This conduct ripen'd all for me and ruin.
Scarce had the priest the holy rites perform'd,
When I, by sacred inspiration, forg'd
That letter which I trusted to thy hand;
That letter, which in glowing terms conveys,
From happy Carlos to fair Leonora,
The most profound acknowledgement of heart,
For wondrous transports which he never knew.

32

This is a good subservient artifice,
To aid the nobler workings of my brain.

Isa. I quickly dropp'd it in the bride's apartment,
As you commanded.

Zan. With a lucky hand;
For soon Alonzo found it; I observ'd him
From out my secret stand. He took it up;
But scarce was it unfolded to his sight,
When he, as if an arrow pierc'd his eye,
Started, and trembling dropp'd it on the ground.
Pale and aghast awhile my victim stood,
Disguis'd a sigh or two, and puff'd them from him;
Then rubb'd his brow and took it up again.
At first he look'd as if he meant to read it;
But check'd by rising fears he crush'd it thus,
And thrust it, like an adder, in his bosom.

Isa. But if he read it not, it cannot sting him,
At least not mortally.

Zan. At first I thought so;
But farther thought informs me otherwise,
And turns this disappointment to account.
This, Isabella, is don Carlos' picture;
Take it, and so dispose of it, that found,
It may raise up a witness of her love;
Under her pillow, in her cabinet,
Or elsewhere, as shall best promote our end.

Isa. I'll weigh it as its consequence requires,
Then do my utmost to deserve your smile.   [*exit.*

Zan. Is that Alonzo prostrate on the ground?—
Now he starts up like flame from sleeping embers,
And wild distraction glares from either eye.
If thus a slight surmise can work his soul,
How will the fulness of the tempest tear him?

Enter Don Alonzo.

Alon. And yet it cannot be—I am deceiv'd—
I injure her: she wears the face of heaven.

Zan. He doubts.　　　　*[aside.*

Alon. I dare not look on this again.
If the first glance, which gave suspicion only,
Had such effect, so smote my heart and brain,
The certainty would dash me all in pieces.
It cannot—Ha! it must, it must be true.　　　*[starts.*

Zan. Hold there, and we succeed. He has descry'd me.
And (for he thinks I love him) will unfold
His aching heart, and rest it on my counsel.
I'll seem to go, to make my stay more sure.　　　*[aside.*

Alon. Hold, Zanga, turn.

Zan. My lord.

Alon. Shut close the doors,
That not a spirit find an entrance here.

Zan. My lord's obey'd.

Alon. I see that thou art frighted.

If thou dost love me, I shall fill thy heart
With scorpions' stings.

Zan. If I do love, my lord?

Alon. Come near me, let me rest upon thy bosom;
(What pillow like the bosom of a friend?)
For I am sick at heart.

Zan. Speak, sir, O, speak,
And take me from the rack.

Alon. I am most happy: mine is victory,
Mine the king's favour, mine the nation's shout,
And great men make their fortunes of my smiles.
O curse of curses! in the lap of blessing
To be most curst!—My Leonora's false!

Zan. Save me, my lord!

Alon. My Leonora's false!   [*gives him the letter.*

Zan. Then heaven has lost its image here on earth.

> [*while Zanga reads the letter, he trembles, and
> shows the utmost concern.*

Alon. Good-natur'd man! he makes my pains his own.
I durst not read it; but I read it now
In thy concern.

Zan. Did you not read it then?

Alon. Mine eye just touch'd it, and could bear no more.

Zan. Thus perish all that gives Alonzo pain! [*tears the letter.*

Alon. Why didst thou tear it?

Zan. Think of it no more.
'Twas your mistake, and groundless are your fears.

Alon. And didst thou tremble then for my mistake?
Or give the whole contents, or by the pangs
That feed upon my heart, thy life's in danger.

Zan. Is this Alonzo's language to his Zanga?
Draw forth your sword, and find the secret here.
For whose sake is it, think you, I conceal it?
Wherefore this rage? Because I seek your peace?
I have no interest in suppressing it,
But what good-natur'd tenderness for you
Obliges me to have. Not mine the heart
That will be rent in two. Not mine the fame
That will be damn'd, though all the world should know it.

Alon. Then my worst fears are true, and life is past.

Zan. What has the rashness of my passion utter'd?
I know not what; but rage is our destruction,
And all its words are wind—Yet sure, I think,
I nothing own'd—but grant I did confess,
What is a letter? letters may be forg'd.

For heav'n's sweet sake, my lord, lift up your heart.
Some foe to your repose—

Alon. So, heaven look on me,
As I can't find the man I have offended.

36

Zan. Indeed! [*aside*]—Our innocence is not our shield.
They take offence, who have not been offended;
They seek our ruin too, who speak us fair,
And death is often ambush'd in their smiles.
'Tis certain
A letter may be forg'd, and in a point
Of such a dreadful consequence as this,
One would rely on nought that might be false—
Think, have you any other cause to doubt her?
Away, you can find none. Resume your spirit;
All's well again.

    Alon. Oh that it were!

    Zan. It is;
For who could credit that, which, credited,
Makes hell superfluous by superior pains,
Without such proofs as cannot be withstood?
Has she not ever been to virtue train'd?
Is not her fame as spotless as the sun,
Her sex's envy, and the boast of Spain?

    Alon. O, Zanga! it is that confounds me most,
That, full in opposition to appearance—

    Zan. No more, my lord, for you condemn yourself.
What is absurdity, but to believe
Against appearance!—You can't yet, I find,
Subdue your passion to your better sense;—
And, truth to tell, it does not much displease me.
'Tis fit our indiscretions should be check'd
With some degree of pain.

Alon. What indiscretion?

Zan. Come, you must bear to hear your faults from me.
Had you not sent don Carlos to the court
The night before the battle, that foul slave,
Who forg'd the senseless scroll which gives you pain,
Had wanted footing for his villany.

Alon. I sent him not.

Zan. Not send him!—Ha!—That strikes me.
I thought he came on message to the king.
Is there another cause could justify
His shunning danger, and the promis'd fight?
But I perhaps may think too rigidly;
So long an absence, and impatient love—

Alon. In my confusion, that had quite escap'd me.
By heaven, my wounded soul does bleed afresh;
'Tis clear as day—for Carlos is so brave,
He lives not but on fame, he hunts for danger,
And is enamour'd of the face of death.
How then could he decline the next day's battle,
But for the transports?—Oh, it must be so—
Inhuman! by the loss of his own honour,
To buy the ruin of his friend!

Zan. You wrong him;
He knew not of your love.

Alon. Ha!—

Zan. That stings home.   [*aside.*

Alon. Indeed, he knew not of my treacherous love—
Proofs rise on proofs, and still the last the strongest.
Love is my torture, love was first my crime;
For she was his, my friend's, and he (O horror!)
Confided all in me. O sacred faith!
How dearly I abide thy violation!

Zan. Were then their loves far gone?

Alon. The father's will
There bore a total sway; and he, as soon
As news arriv'd that Carlos' fleet was seen
From off our coast, fir'd with the love of gold,
Determin'd that the very sun which saw
Carlos' return, should see his daughter wed.

Zan. Indeed, my lord; then you must pardon me,
If I presume to mitigate the crime.
Consider, strong allurements soften guilt;
Long was his absence, ardent was his love,
At midnight his return, the next day destin'd
For his espousals—'twas a strong temptation.

Alon. Temptation!

Zan. 'Twas but gaining of one night.

Alon. One night!

Zan. That crime could ne'er return again.

Alon. Again! By heaven, thou dost insult thy lord.
Temptation! One night gain'd! O stings and death!
And am I then undone? Alas, my Zanga!

And dost thou own it too? Deny it still,
And rescue me one moment from distraction.

Zan. My lord, I hope the best.

Alon. False, foolish hope, thou know'st it false;
It is as glaring as the noon-tide sun.
Devil!—This morning, after three years' coldness,
To rush at once into a passion for me!
'Twas time to feign, 'twas time to get another,
When her first fool was sated with her beauties.

Zan. What says my lord? Did Leonorathen
Never before disclose her passion for you?

Alon. Never.

Zan. Throughout the whole three years?

Alon. O never! never!
Why, Zanga, shouldst thou strive? 'Tis all in vain:
Though thy soul labours, it can find no reed
For hope to catch at. Ah! I'm plunging down
Ten thousand thousand fathoms in despair.

Zan. Hold, sir, I'll break your fall—wave ev'ry fear,
And be a man again—Had he enjoy'd her,

Be most assur'd, he had resign'd her to you
With less reluctance.

Alon. Ha! Resign'd her to me!—
Resign her!—Who resign'd her?—Double death!
How could I doubt so long? My heart is broke.
First love her to distraction! then resign her!

Zan. But was it not with utmost agony?

Alon. Grant that, he still resign'd her; that's enough.
Would he pluck out his eye to give it me?
Tear out his heart?—She was his heart no more—
Nor was it with reluctance he resign'd her;
By heav'n, he ask'd, he courted, me to wed.
I thought it strange; 'tis now no longer so.

Zan. Was't his request? Are you right sure of that?
I fear the letter was not all a tale.

Alon. A tale! There's proof equivalent to sight.

Zan. I should distrust my sight on this occasion.

Alon. And so should I; by heav'n, I think I should.
What, Leonora! the divine, by whom
We guess'd at angels! Oh! I'm all confusion.

Zan. You now are too much ruffled to think clearly.
Since bliss and horror, life and death, hang on it,
Go to your chamber, there maturely weigh
Each circumstance; consider, above all,
That it is jealousy's peculiar nature

To swell small things to great; nay, out of nought
To conjure much, and then to lose its reason
Amid the hideous phantoms it has form'd.

Alon. Had I ten thousand lives, I'd give them all
To be deceiv'd.
And yet she seem'd so pure, that I thought heav'n
Borrow'd her form for virtue's self to wear,

To gain her lovers with the sons of men.
O, Leonora! Leonora!   [*exit.*

Re-enter Isabella.

Zan. Thus far it works auspiciously. My patient
Thrives, underneath my hand, in misery.
He's gone to think; that is, to be distracted.

Isa. I overheard your conference, and saw you,
To my amazement, tear the letter.

Zan. There,
There, Isabella, I out-did myself.
For, tearing it, I not secure it only
In its first force, but superadd a new.
For who can now the character examine
To cause a doubt, much less detect the fraud?
And after tearing it, as loth to show
The foul contents, if I should swear itnow
A forgery, my lord would disbelieve me,
Nay, more, would disbelieve the more I swore.
But is the picture happily dispos'd of?

Isa. It is.

Zan. That's well—Ah! what is well? O pang to think!
O dire necessity! is this my province?
Whither, my soul! ah! whither art thou sunk?
Does this become a soldier? this become
Whom armies follow'd, and a people lov'd?
My martial glory withers at the thought.
But great my end; and since there are no other,
These means are just, they shine with borrow'd light,

42

Illustrious from the purpose they pursue.
    And greater sure my merit, who, to gain
    A point sublime, can such a task sustain;
    To wade through ways obscene, my honour bend,
    And shock my nature, to attain my end.
    Late time shall wonder; that my joys will raise:
    For wonder is involuntary praise.   *[exeunt.*

ACT THE FOURTH.

SCENE I.

Enter Don Alonzo and Zanga.

Alon. Oh, what a pain to think! when ev'ry thought,
Perplexing thought, in intricacies runs,
And reason knits th' inextricable toil,
In which herself is taken!
No more I'll bear this battle of the mind,
This inward anarchy; but find my wife
And, to her trembling heart presenting death,
Force all the secret from her.

    Zan. O, forbear!
You totter on the very brink of ruin.

    Alon. What dost thou mean?

    Zan. That will discover all,
And kill my hopes. What can I think or do?   *[aside.*

    Alon. What, dost thou murmur?

Zan. Force the secret from her!
What's perjury to such a crime as this?
Will she confess it then? O, groundless hope!
But rest assur'd, she'll make this accusation,
Or false or true, your ruin with the king;
Such is her father's pow'r.

Alon. No more, I care not;
Rather than groan beneath this load, I'll die.

Zan. But for what better will you change this load?
Grant you should know it, would not that be worse?

Alon. No; it would cure me of my mortal pangs
By hatred and contempt: I should despise her,
And all my love-bred agonies would vanish.

Zan. Ah! were I sure of that, my lord—

Alon. What then?

Zan. You should not hazard life to gain the secret.

Alon. What dost thou mean? thou know'st I'm on the rack.
I'll not be play'd with; speak, if thou hast aught,
Or I this instant fly to Leonora.

Zan. That is, to death. My lord, I am not yet
Quite so far gone in guilt to suffer it;
Though gone too far, heav'n knows—'Tis I am guilty;
I have took pains, as you, I know, observ'd,
To hinder you from diving in the secret,

And turn'd aside your thoughts from the detection.

Alon. Thou dost confound me.

Zan. I confound myself;
And frankly own, though to my shame I own it,
Nought but your life in danger could have torn
The secret out, and made me own my crime.

Alon. Speak quickly, Zanga, speak.

Zan. Not yet, dread sir:
First, I must be assur'd, that if you find
The fair one guilty, scorn, as you assur'd me,
Shall conquer love and rage, and heal your soul.

Alon. Oh! 't will, by heav'n.

Zan. Alas! I fear it much,
And scarce can hope so far; but I of this
Exact your solemn oath, that you'll abstain
From all self-violence, and save my lord.

Alon. I trebly swear.

Zan. You'll bear it like a man?

Alon. A god.

Zan. Such have you been to me, these tears confess it;
And pour'd forth miracles of kindness on me:
And what amends is now within my pow'r,
But to confess, expose myself to justice,
And as a blessing claim my punishment?
Know then, don Carlos—

Alon. Oh!

Zan. You cannot bear it.

Alon. Go on, I'll have it, though it blast mankind;
I'll have it all, and instantly. Go on.

Zan. Don Carlos did return at dead of night—
That night, by chance (ill chance for me) did I
Command the watch that guards the palace gate.
He told me he had letters for the king,
Despatch'd from you.

Alon. The villain lied!

Zan. My lord,
I pray, forbear—Transported at his sight,
After so long a bondage, and your friend,
(Who could suspect him of an artifice?)
No farther I inquir'd, but let him pass,
False to my trust, at least imprudent in it.
Our watch reliev'd, I went into the garden,
As is my custom, when the night's serene,
And took a moon-light walk: when soon I heard
A rustling in an arbour that was near me.
I saw two lovers in each other's arms,
Embracing and embrac'd. Anon the man
Arose; and, falling back some paces from her,
Gaz'd ardently awhile, then rush'd at once,
And, throwing all himself into her bosom,
There softly sigh'd, "Oh, night of ecstasy!
When shall we meet again?"—Don Carlos then
Led Leonora forth.

Alon. Oh, oh, my heart!   *[he sinks into a chair.*

Zan. Groan on, and with the sound refresh my soul!
'Tis through his heart; his knees smite one another:
'Tis through his brain; his eye-balls roll in anguish.   *[aside.*
My lord, my lord, why will you rack my soul?

Alon. Oh, she was all!
My fame, my friendship, and my love of arms,
All stoop'd to her; my blood was her possession.
Deep in the secret foldings of my heart
She liv'd with life, and far the dearer she:
To think on't is the torment of the damn'd,
And not to think on't is impossible.

Zan. You said you'd bear it like a man.

Alon. I do.
Am I not most distracted?

Zan. Pray, be calm.

Alon. As hurricanes:—be thou assur'd of that.

Zan. Is this the wise Alonzo?

Alon. Villain, no:
He died in the arbour—he was murder'd there!—

Zan. Alas! he weeps.

Alon. Go, dig her grave!

Zan. My lord!

Alon. But that her blood's too hot, I would carouse it
Around my bridal board!

Zan. And I would pledge thee.   [*aside.*

Alon. But I may talk too fast. Pray let me think,
And reason mildly.—Wedded and undone
Before one night descends.—Oh, hasty evil!
What friend to comfort me in my extreme!
Where's Carlos? why is Carlos absent from me?
Does he know what has happen'd?

Zan. My lord!

Alon. Oh, villain, villain, most accurst!
If thou didst know it, why didst let me wed?

Zan. Hear me, my lord; your anger will abate.
I knew it not:—I saw them in the garden;
But saw no more than you might well expect
To see in lovers destin'd for each other.
By heav'n, I thought their meeting innocent.
Who could suspect fair Leonora's virtue,
'Till after-proofs conspir'd to blacken it?
Sad proofs, which came too late, which broke not out,
(Eternal curses on Alvarez' haste!)
'Till holy rites had made the wanton yours;
And then, I own, I labour'd to conceal it,
In duty and compassion to your peace.

Alon. Live now, be damn'd hereafter—for I want thee.
Let me think—

The jess'mine bower—'tis secret and remote:
Go, wait me there, and take thy dagger with thee.   [*exit Zanga.*
How sweet the sound still sings within my ear!
When shall we meet again?—To-night, in hell.   [*going.*

Enter Leonora.

Ha! I'm surprised! I stagger at her charms!
Oh, angel-devil!—Shall I stab her now?
No—It shall be as I at first determin'd.
To kill her now were half my vengeance lost.
Then I must now dissemble—if I can.

   Leon. My lord, excuse me; see, a second time
I come in embassy from all your friends,
Whose joys are languid, uninspir'd by you.

   Alon. This moment, Leonora, I was coming
To thee, and all—but sure, or I mistake,
Or thou canst well inspire my friends with joy.

   Leon. What says my lord?

   Alon. Thou art exceeding fair.

   Leon. Beauty alone is but of little worth;
But when the soul and body of a piece,
Both shine alike; then they obtain a price,
And are a fit reward for gallant actions,
Heaven's pay on earth for such great souls as yours;—
If fair and innocent, I am your due.

   Alon. Innocent!   [*aside.*

Leon. How, my lord! I interrupt you.

Alon. No, my best life! I must not part with thee—
This hand is mine—Oh, what a hand is here!
So soft, souls sink into it, and are lost!

Leon. In tears, my lord?

Alon. What less can speak my joy?
Why, I could gaze upon thy looks for ever,
And drink in all my being from thine eyes;
And I could snatch a flaming thunderbolt,
And hurl destruction!—

Leon. My lord, you fright me.
Is this the fondness of your nuptial hour?
Why, when I woo your hand, is it deny'd me?
Your very eyes, why are they taught to shun me?—
Nay, my good lord, I have a title here,   [*takes his hand.*
And I will have it. Am I not your wife?
Have I not just authority to know
That heart which I have purchas'd with my own?
Tell me the secret; I conjure you, tell me.
Speak then, I charge you speak, or I expire,
And load you with my death. My lord, my lord!

Alon. Ha, ha, ha!
                [*he breaks from her, and she sinks upon the floor.*

Leon. Are these the joys which fondly I conceiv'd?
And is it thus a wedded life begins?
What did I part with, when I gave my heart?
I knew not that all happiness went with it.
Why did I leave my tender father's wing,

And venture into love? The maid that loves,
Goes out to sea upon a shatter'd plank,
And puts her trust in miracles for safety.
Where shall I sigh?—where pour out my complaint?
He that should hear, should succour, should redress,
He is the source of all.

Alon. Go to thy chamber;
I soon will follow; that which now disturbs thee
Shall be clear'd up, and thou shalt not condemn me.
[exit Leonora.
Oh, how like innocence she looks!—What, stab her!
And rush into her blood?
How then? why thus—no more; it is determin'd.

Re-enter Zanga.

Zan. I fear, his heart has fail'd him. She must die.
Can I not rouse the snake that's in his bosom,
To sting out human nature, and effect it?   *[aside.*

Alon. This vast and solid earth, that blazing sun,
Those skies, through which it rolls, must all have end.
What then is man? the smallest part of nothing.
Day buries day; month, month; and year, the year.
Our life is but a chain of many deaths;

Can then death's self be fear'd? our life much rather.
Life is the desert, life the solitude.
Death joins us to the great majority:
'Tis to be borne to Platos and to Cæsars;
'Tis to be great for ever;
'Tis pleasure, 'tis ambition, then to die.

Zan. I think, my lord, you talk'd of death.

Alon. I did.

Zan. I give you joy, then Leonora's dead.

Alon. No, Zanga; to shed a woman's blood
Would stain my sword, and make my wars inglorious;
He who, superior to the checks of nature,
Dares make his life the victim of his reason,
Does in some sort that reason deify,
And take a flight at heaven.

Zan. Alas, my lord,
'Tis not your reason, but her beauty, finds
Those arguments, and throws you on your sword.
You cannot close an eye that is so bright,
You cannot strike a breast that is so soft,
That has ten thousand ecstasies in store—
For Carlos?—No, my lord, I mean foryou.

Alon. Oh, through my heart and marrow! pr'ythee, spare me,
Nor more upbraid the weakness of thy lord:
I own, I try'd, I quarrell'd with my heart,
And push'd it on, and bid it give herdeath;
But, oh, her eyes struck first and murder'd me.

Zan. I know not what to answer to my lord.
Men are but men; we did not make ourselves.
Farewell then, my best lord, since you must die.
Oh, that I were to share your monument,
And in eternal darkness close these eyes
Against those scenes which I am doom'd to suffer!

Alon. What dost thou mean?

Zan. And is it then unknown?
Oh, grief of heart, to think that you should ask it!
Sure you distrust that ardent love I bear you,
Else could you doubt when you are laid in dust—
But it will cut my poor heart through and through,
To see those revel on your sacred tomb,
Who brought you thither by their lawless loves.
For there they'll revel, and exult to find
Him sleep so fast, who else might mar their joys.

Alon. Distraction! But don Carlos well thou know'st
Is sheath'd in steel, and bent on other thoughts.

Zan. I'll work him to the murder of his friend.   [*aside.*
Yes, till the fever of his blood returns,
While her last kiss still glows upon his cheek.
But when he finds Alonzo is no more,
How will he rush, like lightning, to her arms!
There sigh, there languish, there pour out his soul;
But not in grief—sad obsequies to thee!—
But thou wilt be at peace, nor see, nor hear,
The burning kiss, the sigh of ecstasy,
Their throbbing hearts that jostle one another:
Thank heaven, these torments will be all my own.

Alon. I'll ease thee of that pain. Let Carlos die;
O'ertake him on the road, and see it done.
'Tis my command.   [*gives his signet.*

Zan. I dare not disobey.

Alon. My Zanga, now I have thy leave to die.

53

Zan. Ah, sir! think, think again. Are all men buried
In Carlos' grave? you know not womankind:
When once the throbbing of the heart has broke
The modest zone, with which it first was ty'd,
Each man she meets will be a Carlos to her.

Alon. That thought has more of hell than had the former.
Another, and another, and another!
And each shall cast a smile upon my tomb.
I am convinc'd; I must not, will not, die.

Zan. You cannot die; nor can you murder her.
What then remains? In nature no third way,
But to forget, and so to love again.

Alon. Oh!

Zan. If you forgive, the world will call you good;
If you forget, the world will call you wise;
If you receive her to your grace again,
The world will call you—very, very kind.

Alon. Zanga, I understand thee well. She dies;
Though my arm tremble at the stroke, she dies.

Zan. That's truly great. What think you 'twas set up
The Greek and Roman name in such a lustre,
But doing right in stern despite to nature;
Shutting their ears to all her little cries,
When great, august, and godlike justice call'd?
At Aulis, one pour'd out a daughter's life,
And gain'd more glory than by all his wars;
Another, slew a sister in just rage;
A third, the theme of all succeeding times,

Gave to the cruel axe a darling son:
Nay more, for justice some devote themselves,
As he at Carthage, an immortal name!
Yet there is one step left above them all,
Above their history, above their fable:
A wife, bride, mistress, unenjoy'd—do that,
And tread upon the Greek and Roman glory.

    Alon. 'Tis done!—Again new transports fire my brain:
I had forgot it, 'tis my bridal night.
Friend, give me joy, we must be gay together;
See that the festival be duly honour'd.
       And when with garlands the full bowl is crown'd,
       And music gives her elevating sound,
       And golden carpets spread the sacred floor,
       And a new day the blazing tapers pour,
       Thou, Zanga, then my solemn friends invite,
       From the dark realms of everlasting night;
       Call Vengeance, call the furies, call Despair,
       And Death, our chief-invited guest, be there;
       He, with pale hand, shall lead the bride, and spread
       Eternal curtains round our nuptial bed.   [*exeunt.*

ACT THE FIFTH.

SCENE I.

Enter Alonzo, meeting Zanga.

Alon. Is Carlos murder'd?

Zan. I obey'd your order.
Six ruffians overtook him on the road;
He fought as he was wont, and four he slew.
Then sunk beneath an hundred wounds to death.
His last breath blest Alonzo, and desir'd
His bones might rest near yours.

Alon. Oh, Zanga! Zanga!
But I'll not think: for I must act, and thinking
Would ruin me for action.
Where's Leonora then? Quick, answer me:
I'm deep in horrors, I'll be deeper still.
I find thy artifice did take effect,
And she forgives my late deportment to her.

Zan. I told her, from your childhood you was wont,
On any great surprise, but chiefly then
When cause of sorrow bore it company,
To have your passion shake the seat of reason;
A momentary ill, which soon blew o'er:
Then did I tell her of don Carlos' death
(Wisely suppressing by what means he fell),
And laid the blame on that. At first she doubted;
But such the honest artifice I us'd,
And such her ardent wish it should be true,
That she, at length, was fully satisfied.
But what design you, sir, and how?

Alon. I'll tell thee.
Thus I've ordain'd it. In the jess'mine bow'r,
The place which she dishonour'd with her guilt,

There will I meet her; the appointment's made;
And calmly spread (for I can do it now)
The blackness of her crime before her sight;
And then, with all the cool solemnity
Of public justice, give her to the grave.   [*exit.*

Zan. Why, get thee gone! horror and night go with thee.
Sisters of Acheron, go hand in hand,
Go dance around the bow'r, and close them;
And tell them, that I sent you to salute them
Profane the ground; and for th' ambrosial rose,
And breath of jess'mine, let hemlock blacken,
And deadly nightshade poison, all the air.
For the sweet nightingale, may ravens croak,
Toads pant, and adders rustle through the leaves;
May serpents winding up the trees let fall
Their hissing necks upon them from above,
And mingle kisses—such as I would give them.   [*exit.*

SCENE II. THE BOWER.

Enter Alonzo.—Leonora sleeping.

Alon. Ye amaranths! ye roses, like the morn!
Sweet myrtles, and ye golden orange groves!
Why do you smile? Why do you look so fair?
Are ye not blighted as I enter in?
Did ever midnight ghosts assemble here?
Have these sweet echoes ever learn'd to groan?
Joy-giving, love-inspiring, holy bow'r!
Know, in thy fragrant bosom thou receiv'st
A—murderer! Oh, I shall stain thy lilies,
And horror will usurp the seat of bliss.   [*advances.*
Ha! she sleeps—

The day's uncommon heat has overcome her.
Then take, my longing eyes, your last, full gaze.
Oh, what a sight is here! how dreadful fair!
Who would not think that being innocent?
Where shall I strike? who strikes her, strikes himself.
My own life-blood will issue at her wound.
But see, she smiles! I never shall smile more;
It strongly tempts me to a parting kiss.   [*going, he starts back.*
Ha! smile again. She dreams of him she loves.
Curse on her charms! I'll stab her through them all.
                              [*as he is going to strike, she wakes.*

Leon. My lord, your stay was long; and yonder lull
Of falling waters tempted me to rest,
Dispirited with noon's excessive heat.

Alon. Ye pow'rs! with what an eye she mends the day!
While they were clos'd, I should have giv'n the blow.   [*aside.*

Leon. What says my lord?

Alon. Why, this Alonzo says:
If love were endless, men were gods; 'tis that
Does counterbalance travel, danger, pain—
'Tis heav'n's expedient to make mortals bear
The light, and cheat them of the peaceful grave.

Leon. Alas, my lord! why talk you of the grave?
Your friend is dead: in friendship you sustain
A mighty loss; repair it with my love.

Alon. Thy love, thou piece of witchcraft! I would say,
Thou brightest angel! I could gaze for ever.
But oh, those eyes! those murderers! Oh, whence,

Whence didst thou steal their burning orbs? from heaven?
Thou didst; and 'tis religion to adore them.

Leon. My best Alonzo, moderate your thoughts.
Extremes still fright me, though of love itself.

Alon. Extremes indeed! it hurry'd me away;
But I come home again—and now for justice—
And now for death—It is impossible—   [*aside.*
I leave her to just heav'n.   [*drops the dagger, goes off.*

Leon. Ha, a dagger!
What dost thou say, thou minister of death?
What dreadful tale dost tell me?—Let me think—

Enter Zanga.

Zan. Death to my tow'ring hope! Oh! fall from high!
My close, long-labour'd scheme at once is blasted,
That dagger, found, will cause her to inquire;
Inquiry will discover all; my hopes
Of vengeance perish; I myself am lost—
Curse on the coward's heart; wither his hand,
Which held the steel in vain!—what can be done?
Where can I fix?—that's something still—'twill breed
Fell rage and bitterness betwixt their souls,
Which may, perchance, grow up to greater evil:
If not, 'tis all I can—It shall be so—   [*aside.*

Leon. Oh, Zanga, I am sinking in my fears!
Alonzo dropp'd this dagger as he left me,
And left me in a strange disorder too.
What can this mean? Angels preserve his life!

Zan. Yours, madam, yours.

Leon. What, Zanga, dost thou say?

Zan. Carry you goodness then to such extremes,
So blinded to the faults of him you love,
That you perceive not he is jealous?

Leon. Heav'ns!
And yet a thousand things recur that swear it.
What villain could inspire him with that thought?
It is not of the growth of his own nature.

Zan. Some villain; who, hell knows; but he is jealous;
And 'tis most fit a heart so pure as yours
Do itself justice, and assert its honour,
And make him conscious of his stab to virtue.

Leon. Jealous! it sickens at my heart. Unkind,
Ungen'rous, groundless, weak, and insolent!
Why, wherefore? on what shadow of occasion?
Oh, how the great man lessens to my thought!
How could so mean a vice as jealousy
Live in a throng of such exalted virtues! I
scorn and hate, yet love him, and adore. I
cannot, will not, dare not, think it true,
'Till from himself I know it.   [*exit.*

Zan. This succeeds
Just to my wish. Now she, with violence,
Upbraids him; he, not doubting she is guilty,
Rages no less; and if on either side
The waves run high, there still lives hope of ruin.

60

Re-enter Alonzo.

My lord—

Alon. Oh, Zanga, hold thy peace! I am no coward;
But heav'n itself did hold my hand; I felt it,
By the well-being of my soul, I did.
I'll think of vengeance at another season.

Zan. My lord, her guilt—

Alon. Perdition on thee, Moor,
For that one word! Ah, do not rouse that thought!
I have o'erwhelm'd it much as possible:
I tell thee, Moor, I love her to distraction.
If 'tis my shame, why, be it so—I love her;
I could not hurt her to be lord of earth;
It shocks my nature like a stroke from heav'n.
But see, my Leonora comes—Be gone.   [*exit Zanga.*

Re-enter Leonora.

Oh, seen for ever, yet for ever new!
The conquer'd thou dost conquer o'er again,
Inflicting wound on wound.

Leon. Alas, my lord!
What need of this to me?

Alon. Ha! dost thou weep?

Leon. Have I no cause?

Alon. If love is thy concern,

61

Thou hast no cause: none ever lov'd like me.
Oh, that this one embrace would last for ever!

Leon. Could this man ever mean to wrong my virtue?
Could this man e'er design upon my life?
Impossible! I throw away the thought.   [*aside.*
These tears declare how much I taste the joy
Of being folded in your arms and heart;
My universe does lie within that space.
This dagger bore false witness.

Alon. Ha, my dagger!
It rouses horrid images. Away,
Away with it, and let us talk of love.

Leon. Of death!

Alon. As thou lov'st happiness—

Leon. Of murder!

Alon. Rash,
Rash woman! yet forbear.
Alas, thou quite mistak'st my cause of pain!
Yet, yet dismiss me; I am all in flames.

Leon. Who has most cause, you or myself? what act
Of my whole life encourag'd you to this?
Or of your own, what guilt has drawn it on you?
You find me kind, and think me kind to all;
The weak, ungen'rous error of your sex.
What could inspire the thought? We oft'nest judge
From our own hearts; and is yours then so frail,
It prompts you to conceive thus ill of me?

He that can stoop to harbour such a thought,
Deserves to find it true.   [*holding him.*

Alon. [*turning on her*] Ill-fated woman!
Why hast thou forc'd me back into the gulf
Of agonies I had block'd up from thought?
For, since thou hast replung'd me in my torture,
I will be satisfy'd.

Leon. Be satisfy'd!

Alon. Yes, thy own mouth shall witness it against
thee; I will be satisfy'd.

Leon. Of what?

Alon. Of what?
How dar'st thou ask that question? Woman, woman,
Weak and assur'd at once! thus 'tis for ever.
Who told thee that thy virtue was suspected?
Who told thee I design'd upon thy life?
You found the dagger; but that could not speak:
Nor did I tell thee; who did tell thee then?
Guilt, conscious guilt!

Leon. This to my face! Oh, heaven!

Alon. This to thy very soul.

Leon. Thou'rt not in earnest?

Alon. Serious as death.

Leon. Then heav'n have mercy on thee.

Till now, I struggled not to think it true;
I sought conviction, and would not believe it.
And dost thou force me? this shall not be borne
Thou shalt repent this insult.   [*going.*

   Alon. Madam, stay.
Your passion's wise; 'tis a disguise for guilt:
You and your thousand arts shall not escape me.

   Leon. Arts?

   Alon. Arts! Confess; for death is in my hand.

   Leon. 'Tis in your words.

   Alon. Confess, confess, confess!
Nor tear my veins with passion to compel thee.

   Leon. I scorn to answer thee, presumptuous man!

   Alon. Deny then, and incur a fouler shame.
Where did I find this picture?

   Leon. Ha, don Carlos!
By my best hopes, more welcome than thy own.

   Alon. I know it; but is vice so very rank,
That thou shouldst dare to dash it in my face?

Nature is sick of thee, abandon'd woman!

   Leon. Repent.

   Alon. Is that for me?

Leon. Fall, ask my pardon.

Alon. Astonishment!

Leon. Dar'st thou persist to think I am dishonest?

Alon. I know thee so.

Leon. This blow then to thy heart—
                    [*she stabs herself; he endeavours to prevent her.*

Alon. Ho, Zanga! Isabella! ho! she bleeds!
Descend, ye blessed angels, to assist her!

Leon. This is the only way I would wound thee,
Though most unjust. Now think me guilty still.

Enter Isabella.

Alon. Bear her to instant help. The world to save her.

Leon. Unhappy man! well may'st thou gaze and tremble.
But fix thy terror and amazement right;
Not on my blood, but on thy own distraction.
What hast thou done? whom censur'd—Leonora!
When thou hadst censur'd, thou wouldst save her life:
Oh, inconsistent! should I live in shame,
Or stoop to any other means but this
T' assert my virtue? no: she who disputes,
Admits it possible she might be guilty.
While aught but truth could be my inducement to it,
While it might look like an excuse to thee,
I scorn'd to vindicate my innocence:
But now, I let thy rashness know, the wound

Which least I feel, is that my dagger made.

[*exit Isabella, leading out Leonora.*

Alon. Ha! was this woman guilty?—And if not—
How my thoughts darken that way! grant, kind heaven,
That she prove guilty; or my being end.
Is that my hope, then?—Sure, the sacred dust
Of her that bore me trembles in its urn.

Is it in man the sore distress to bear,
When hope itself is blacken'd to despair?
When all the bliss I pant for, is to gain
In hell, a refuge from severer pain?   [*exit.*

Re-enter Zanga.

Zan. How stands the great account 'twixt me and vengeance?
Though much is paid, yet still it owes me much,
And I will not abate a single groan—
Ha! that were well—but that were fatal too—
Why, be it so—Revenge so truly great,
Would come too cheap, if bought with less than life.

Re-enter Isabella.

Isa. Ah, Zanga, see me tremble! has not yet

Thy cruel heart its fill?—Poor Leonora—

Zan. Welters in blood, and gasps for her last breath.
What then? we all must die.

Isa. Alonzo raves,
And, in the tempest of his grief, has thrice
Attempted on his life. At length, disarm'd,
He calls his friends, that save him, his worst foes,

And importunes the skies for swift perdition.
Thus in his storm of sorrow: after pause,
He started up, and call'd aloud for Zanga,
For Zanga rav'd; and see, he seeks you here,
To learn the truth which most he dreads to know.

Zan. Begone. Now, now, my soul, consummate all.

[*exit Isabella.*

Re-enter Alonzo.

Alon. Oh, Zanga!

Zan. Do not tremble so; but speak.

Alon. I dare not.   [*falls on him.*

Zan. You will drown me with your tears.

Alon. Have I not cause?

Zan. As yet, you have no cause.

Alon. Dost thou too rave?

Zan. Your anguish is to come:
You much have been abus'd.

Alon. Abus'd! by whom?

Zan. To know, were little comfort.

Alon. Oh, 'twere much!

Zan. Indeed!

Alon. By heaven! Oh, give him to my fury!

Zan. Born for your use, I live but to oblige you.
Know, then, 'twas—I.

Alon. Am I awake?

Zan. For ever.
Thy wife is guiltless—that's one transport to me;
And I, I let thee know it—that's another.
I urg'd don Carlos to resign his mistress,
I forg'd the letter, I dispos'd the picture;
I hated, I despis'd, and I destroy!

Alon. Oh!   [*swoons.*

Zan. Why, this is well—why, this is blow for blow!
Where are you? crown me, shadow me with laurels,
Ye spirits which delight in just revenge!
Let Europe and her pallid sons go weep;
Let Afric and her hundred thrones rejoice:
Oh, my dear countrymen, look down and see
How I bestride your prostrate conqueror!
I tread on haughty Spain, and all her kings.
But this is mercy, this is my indulgence;
'Tis peace, 'tis refuge from my indignation.
I must awake him into horrors. Hoa!
Alonzo, hoa! the Moor is at the gate!
Awake, invincible, omnipotent!
Thou who dost all subdue!

Alon. Inhuman slave!

Zan. Fall'n Christian, thou mistak'st my character.
Look on me. Who am I? I know, thou say'st
The Moor, a slave, an abject, beaten slave:
(Eternal woes to him that made me so!)
But look again. Has six years' cruel bondage
Extinguish'd majesty so far, that nought
Shines here to give an awe of one above thee?
When the great Moorish king, Abdallah, fell,
Fell by thy hand accurs'd, I fought fast by him,
His son, though, through his fondness, in disguise,
Less to expose me to th' ambitious foe.—
Ha! does it wake thee?—O'er my father's corse
I stood astride till I had clove thy crest;
And then was made the captive of a squadron,
And sunk into thy servant—But, oh! what,
What were my wages? Hear not heaven, nor earth!
My wages were a blow! by heaven, a blow!
And from a mortal hand!

Alon. Oh, villain, villain!

Zan. All strife is vain.   [*showing a dagger.*

Alon. Is thus my love return'd?
Is this my recompense? Make friends of tigers!

Lay not your young, oh, mothers, on the breast,
For fear they turn to serpents as they lie,
And pay you for their nourishment with death!—
Carlos is dead, and Leonora dying!
Both innocent, both murder'd, both by me.

Zan. Must I despise thee too, as well as hate thee?
Complain of grief, complain thou art a man.—
Priam from fortune's lofty summit fell;

Great Alexander 'midst his conquests mourn'd;
Heroes and demi-gods have known their sorrows;
Cæsars have wept; and I have had—my blow:
But, 'tis reveng'd, and now my work is done.
Yet, ere I fall, be it one part of vengeance
To force thee to confess that I am just.—
Thou seest a prince, whose father thou hast slain,
Whose native country thou hast laid in blood,
Whose sacred person (oh!) thou hast profan'd,
Whose reign extinguish'd—what was left to me,
So highly born? No kingdom, but revenge;
No treasure, but thy tortures and thy groans.
If men should ask who brought thee to thy end,
Tell them, the Moor, and they will not despise thee.
If cold white mortals censure this great deed,
Warn them, they judge not of superior beings,
Souls made of fire, and children of the sun,
With whom revenge is virtue. Fare thee well—
Now, fully satisfied, I should take leave:
But one thing grieves me, since thy death is near,
I leave thee my example how to die.

As he is going to stab himself, Alonzo rushes upon him to prevent him.
In the mean time, enter Don Alvarez, attended. They disarm and
seize Zanga, Alonzo puts the dagger in his bosom.

Alon. No, monster, thou shalt not escape by death.

Oh, father!

Alv. Oh, Alonzo!—Isabella,
Touch'd with remorse to see her mistress' pangs,
Told all the dreadful tale.

Alon. What groan was that?

Zan. As I have been a vulture to thy heart,
So will I be a raven to thine ear,
As true as ever snuff'd the scent of blood,
As ever flapp'd its heavy wing against
The window of the sick, and croak'd despair.
Thy wife is dead.   [*Alvarez goes aside, and returns.*

Alv. The dreadful news is true.

Alon. Prepare the rack; invent new torments for him.

Zan. This too is well. The fix'd and noble mind
Turns all occurrence to its own advantage;
And I'll make vengeance of calamity.
Were I not thus reduc'd, thou wouldst not know,
That, thus reduc'd, I dare defy thee still.
Torture thou may'st, but thou shall ne'er despise me.
The blood will follow where the knife is driven,
The flesh will quiver where the pincers tear,
And sighs and cries by nature grow on pain.
But these are foreign to the soul: not mine
The groans that issue, or the tears that fall;
They disobey me; on the rack I scorn thee,
As when my falchion clove thy helm in battle.

Alv. Peace, villain!

Zan. While I live, old man, I'll speak.
And, well I know, thou dar'st not kill me yet;
For that would rob thy blood-hounds of their prey.

Alon. Who call'd Alonzo?

Alv. No one call'd, my son.

71

Alon. Again!—'Tis Carlos' voice, and I obey.
Oh, how I laugh at all that this can do!   [*shows dagger.*
The wounds that pain'd, the wounds that murder'd me,
Were giv'n before; I am already dead;
This only marks my body for the grave.   [*stabs himself.*
Afric, thou art reveng'd.—Oh, Leonora!   [*dies.*

Zan. Good ruffians, give me leave; my blood is yours,
The wheel's prepar'd, and you shall have it all.
Let me but look one moment on the dead,
And pay yourselves with gazing on my pangs.
                    [*he goes to Alonzo's body.*
Is this Alonzo? Where's the haughty mien?
Is that the hand which smote me? Heavens, how pale!
And art thou dead? So is my enmity.
I war not with the dust. The great, the proud,
The conqueror of Afric was my foe.
A lion preys not upon carcases.
This was thy only method to subdue me.
Terror and doubt fall on me: all thy good

Now blazes, all thy guilt is in the grave.
Never had man such funeral applause:
If I lament thee, sure thy worth was great.
Oh, vengeance, I have follow'd thee too far,
And to receive me, hell blows all her fires.   [*exeunt.*

THE END.

─────

Mr. Hughes, in his criticism on *Othello*, introduces the following narrative,
to which allusion is made in our remarks.—"The short story I am going to tell

is a just warning to those of jealous honour to look about them, and begin to possess their souls as they ought; for no man of spirit knows how terrible a creature he is, till he comes to be provoked.

"Don Alonzo, a Spanish nobleman, had a beautiful and virtuous wife, with whom he had lived some years in great tranquillity. The gentleman, however, was not free from the faults usually imputed to his nation; he was proud, suspicious, and impetuous. He kept a Moor in his house, whom, on a complaint from his lady, he had punished for a small offence with the utmost severity. The slave vowed revenge, and communicated his resolution to one of the lady's women, with whom he had lived in a criminal way. This creature also hated her mistress, for she feared she was observed by her; she therefore undertook to make Don Alonzo jealous, by insinuating that the gardner was often admitted to his lady in private, and promising to make him an eye witness of it. At a proper time, agreed on between her and the Morisco, she sent a message to the gardner, that his lady, having some hasty orders to give him, would have him come that moment to her in her chamber. In the mean time she had placed Alonzo privately in an outer room, that he might observe who passed that way. It was not long before he saw the gardner appear. Alonzo had not patience, but following him into the apartment, struck him at one blow with a dagger to the heart; then dragging his lady by the hair, without inquiring farther, he instantly killed her.

"Here he paused, looking on the dead bodies with all the agitations of a demon of revenge; when the wench who had occasioned these terrors, distracted with remorse, threw herself at his feet, and in a voice of lamentation, without sense of the consequence, repeated all her guilt. Alonzo was overwhelmed with the violent passions at one instant, and uttered the broken voices and motions of each of them for a moment; till at last he recollected himself enough to end his agony of love, anger, disdain, revenge, and remorse, by murdering the maid, the Moor, and himself."

Maurice,
Fenchurch Street.